TO MY NEPHEW AND NIECE,
AXEL AND AUTUMN DEAN.

www.mascotbooks.com

Itty-Bitty Bentlee

For more information, please contact:
Mascot Books, an imprint of Amplify Publishing Group
620 Herndon Parkway, Suite 320
Herndon, VA 20170
info@mascotbooks.com

Library of Congress Control Number: 2022903076

CPSIA Code: PRT0522A

ISBN-13: 978-1-63755-438-8

Printed in the United States

Itty-Bitty Bentlee

by
Julie Wagg

Illustrated by Norris Hall

You're about to meet . . .

an itty-bitty,
little-tiny,
teeny-weeny,
skinny-mini . . .

Yorkie Maltese Poodle named . . .

BENTLEE

Itty-Bitty Bentlee has **SILKY, GRAYISH** hair.
He's a snuggle-bug, fun-to-hug,
furry cuddle bear.

Itty-Bitty Bentlee has **ITTY-BITTY** brown eyes.

They're teeny when he's sleepy, but for treats . . . they open **WIDE!**

Itty-Bitty Bentlee has a **LITTLE-TINY** nose.

It's black, always wet,
and can even touch his toes!

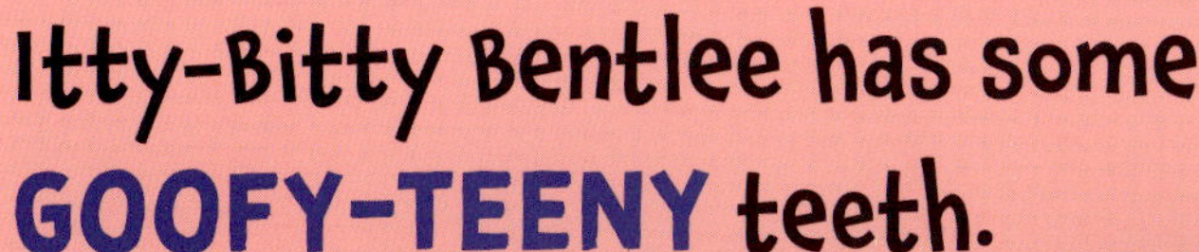

Itty-Bitty Bentlee has some **GOOFY-TEENY** teeth.

They play peek-a-boo,
popping out from underneath!

Itty-Bitty Bentlee's head is shaped just like a heart.

His **REAL BIG** ears . . . are the not-so-tiny part.

Itty-Bitty Bentlee has a **TEENY-WEENY** tail . . .

with fur that makes a curl, just like the swirl of a snail!

Itty-Bitty Bentlee has super stylish taste . . .

lots of clothes that barely fit his **SKINNY-MINI** waist.

Itty-Bitty Bentlee loves to chase his yellow ball.

He's faster than a lightning bolt—
his legs are **EXTRA TALL!**

Itty-Bitty Bentlee is a
ONE-OF-A-KIND guy,
who struts around
in bow ties . . .
he isn't very shy.

Itty-Bitty Bentlee's size **NEVER** gets him down.

He prances right up to the **BIG DOGS** in town!

So to keep him safe and sound,

never lost . . .

and always found . . .

This itty-bitty,
little-tiny,
teeny-weeny,
skinny-mini . . .

wears a sparkly silver collar!

Can Itty-Bitty Bentlee get any smaller?

Goodbye, my friends,
goodbye for now,
but not for very long.

I'm off to Camp Gammy and Gampy—
I hope you'll come along!

JULIE MARIE WAGG lives in California with her partner, Cecilia, and their beloved dog, Bentlee. Julie has worked as a dog groomer for the past sixteen years. Once she created Bentlee's heart-shaped head, she knew this was his signature style. Bentlee reopened the creative side of her mind to the world of writing, but this time with children's books. *Itty-Bitty Bentlee* is her first completed children's book, and she hopes for many more to come.

Julie takes Bentlee everywhere she goes. They wake up cuddling, go on daily adventures, and most importantly, she takes tons of pictures for his Instagram. The close bond Julie and Bentlee have is the best gift she's ever been given. Her goal for this book is for families to enjoy time together, to smile, laugh, and love. Every moment is priceless and precious, and that's why Julie spends as much time with Bentlee as possible.

@ITTYBITTYBENTLEE
#ITTYBITTYBENTLEE
EMAIL: ITTYBITTYBENTLEE@GMAIL.COM